The Day The Music Died

An Emlyn Goode Mystery

Susan Lynn Solomon

Solstice Publishing -
www.solsticepublishing.com

The Day The Music Died
An Emlyn Goode Mystery

Susan Lynn Solomon

To Anna,
A new friend.

Susan Lynn Solomon

For Gary Copeland, a dear friend lost too
soon.
Each of us blessed to have known him
are better people for being welcomed into
his heart.

Prologue

I knew *of* her, of course, though I had never met her. Amanda Stone, the rock and roll queen, was born and raised in my western New York city. At seven, she began her lessons at Miss Bev's Dance Studio on Pine Avenue. Perhaps that was why she moved on the stage with such grace and ease. In her fifth grade music class, she learned to play the violin. She traded that instrument for a guitar when she entered Niagara Falls High School (eight local rock musicians claimed credit for teaching her), and performed with a couple of local bands. After graduation, she left Niagara Falls for a downstate college. A year later, she began to play songs she wrote at open-mics in Greenwich Village, and soon was booked regularly at the *Other End* on Bleeker Street. After her performance one April night, she met Bobby Davis, a struggling bass player. As reported on Page Six of the *New York Post*, "Within the cacophony of raised voices and clinking clatter of glasses, Stone and Davis talked for hours. By evening's end, they'd found their soulmates."

The two formed a band and called it Stonemaiden. In less than six months, the band signed a contract with SONY Records, and within two years their songs with paranormal themes thrilled crowds in sold-out stadiums. Paraphrasing an old lyric, Stonemaiden was a skyrocket in flight.

There's a problem with skyrockets, though. They tend to crash to earth and burn.

Rumors soon spread. *Billboard* and *Cash Box,* two music industry trade publications, reported on drugs, alcohol, and wild parties before and after Stonemaiden appearances. Amanda Stone, they reported, was at the heart of those orgies. In and out of the industry, people began to refer to her as "the Stoned Maiden." At last, during a September 1986 concert in Chicago's Grant Park, her voice began to quiver. Then her body did. In the middle of the group's set, she walked off the stage and, quite literally, disappeared. If anyone ever found out why she did or where she went, it was never reported. Rumor had it that Stone and the band had recorded a new album before she vanished. If they had, it was never released. According to their manager, Eric Riley, the band tried to continue with-out Stone. But, lacking her voice on a new album, their stardom faded. In a year, Stone, Davis, and the band became yesterday's news; their songs played on oldie stations.

The mystery of Stone's disappearance was dredged up recently, after an enterprising *Niagara Gazette* reporter got word she had moved back to her home town. When the story appeared in the newspaper, it meant little to me. My mother had been killed several weeks earlier. Rebecca Nurse and I were in the hospital. I briefly discussed our local celebrity with Rebecca, and then forgot about her. That is, until the mail was delivered almost two weeks after my mother's death. The sympathy card I received was benign. What it led to threw my life into turmoil.

Chapter One
A Sympathy Note

Rebecca and I had just been released from Memorial Hospital after a beating we had taken at the hands of Roger Frey's estranged wife. Rebecca's kneecap had been broken, and I had a couple of cracked ribs. Why Judith Frey attacked us with a baseball bat is another story—one I plan to write one day. Suffice it to say, my friend and I were far from mobile. As a result, Roger and his boss, Detective Chief Harry Woodward, urged Rebecca to stay at my house where she'd be closer to the medical treatment she'd need.

Entirely logical, right?

Not quite. Early on, Rebecca and I decided the guys actually wanted us close enough to keep an eye on. I must admit their concern wasn't entirely misplaced. I had a penchant for getting close to murders and dragging my friend along with me. But, that was in the past. I thought.

Anyway, that Wednesday morning we were in my kitchen. Roger, the Deputy Detective Chief of the Niagara Falls Police Department, had taken on the role of our nursemaid, and had fixed us toast and eggs for breakfast.

Tall, with a square jaw, chiseled cheekbones, and a slightly cleft chin, this man was my neighbor and more than a dear friend. Of course, it wasn't only his good looks (not to mention his rather large hands and size fourteen shoes) that drew me to him. More than once this guy had saved me... well, from myself.

He was at the counter pouring coffee into white mugs, while in our bathrobes, Rebecca and I sat at the round dinette table trying to decipher a passage in the book that had passed through generations of the Goode family. This book had been started by my ancient relative sometime in the 1690s. It was her diary, and at the same time, a cook-book... of a sort. You see, in it were the recipes that had gotten old Sarah Goode hanged in Salem.

I sighed and pushed the book in front of my friend. "The ink looks more faded than when my mother sent this to me. Is there anything in your shop that'll preserve it?"

Rebecca owns *The Black Cat*, an arcane shop in Ellicottville, a town fifty miles south of Niagara Falls. In her shop are herbs that cooks haven't used in centuries, and books which teach skills which three-hundred-twenty years ago would have had women accused of tangoing with Satan.

My friend shook her head. "I'm afraid there's nothing that can save this."

From the sink where Roger was filling the pot to brew more coffee, he said, "Why don't you copy everything in the book onto your computer?"

We both looked at him.

"Good idea," Rebecca said.

Roger's grin showed the gap between his front teeth. "I get one of those once in a while. In fact, since the two of you are stuck in the house, why not make a project of it?"

Roger was one of the few people who knew what was in old Sarah's book.

"Do you think we could?" I asked Rebecca.

She tossed her long salt and pepper braid over her shoulder, and lifted the book to examine the faded letters. As she started to answer, we heard a knock on the screen door.

"Everybody dressed?" Harry Woodward called from the front stoop.

"About as dressed as these two characters get these days," Roger said.

Rebecca pushed herself up from her chair, grabbed her crutches, and hobbled from the kitchen. A few minutes later she came back, but wasn't hobbling. Harry, who had gray hair cut as short as it had been when he was a Marine Colonel, and stood six and a half feet from the ground, was holding her crutches and almost carrying her.

I had no idea when these two became what gossip columns would call "an item". Harry had taken a leave of absence after his wife was killed, and when he returned almost a year later, he and Rebecca were together. Not once in all that time had my dear best friend said a word about it.

Roger filled a mug with coffee and brought it to his boss at the white dinette table. Have I mentioned that my kitchen was entirely white? The cupboards, counters, appliances—even the microwave and coffee pot were white. I'm nothing if not consistent.

Harry raised the mug to his lips, then immediately put it down. "Oh, I nearly forgot," he said, and glanced at Rebecca who sat next to him with dreamy, schoolgirl smile. He patted her hand, then reached into the pocket of his gray sport coat, and pulled out half a dozen envelopes. "I stopped at the mailbox on my way in."

Five of these were window envelopes, clearly bills. The other, much smaller, looked as if it contained a card of some kind.

"Who's it from?" Roger asked. This cop had a nosy streak wider than the Niagara gorge.

I looked at the neatly printed return address, and my eyes narrowed. "Amanda Stone."

"Amanda..." Rebecca said. "Let me see!" She snatched the envelope from my hand. "It is." She showed it to Harry, then to Roger. "It's from Amanda Stone." She gave it back to me. "You got a letter from Amanda Stone." Her eyes rolled up. "What's it say?"

I couldn't help but laugh. In all the time we'd been friends, I'd ever known Rebecca to be star-struck.

A white head with very pink eyes, poked around the door to the kitchen, obviously drawn by the excitement. This was Elvira, the hefty albino cat that had followed me home from my friend's shop several years ago. Since then, the snoopy pain in my derriere had made a nest in my home and my life. Not that I minded. This cat had often been an aider-and-abettor when I had a bright idea. Of course, sometimes those ideas caused me to stroll into the kind of trouble Roger constantly pulled me out of.

As she ambled into the kitchen, Elvira mewed, *Well, what does the letter say?*

I didn't know whether that's what the cat said—I'm a writer, you see, and have a rather vivid imagination. I told her, "Give me a second!"

I opened the envelope, read the card to myself, then read it again aloud.

> *"I just saw the obituary for Anne Goode. I'm sorry to hear of her passing. I knew her a long time ago—she was Annie Bishop then. I was quite fond of her, and hoped to speak with her now that I've returned to Niagara Falls. Since that can no longer be, I would very much like to meet you, Emlyn, and share a few memories of her. Please call me."*

Amanda Stone had written her phone number at the bottom of the condolence note.

Rebecca stood behind me while I read. Now, she rested one of her crutches against my chair, and again pulled the card from my hand. Holding it out, she said, "Of course, you're going to see her." Leaning against my shoulder, my friend bent over to look at my face. "You are, aren't you?"

I glanced at Roger, who shrugged his broad shoulders.

"I don't see why not," he said.

"Sounds like a good idea to me," Harry added, and looked at Roger. "It might make a nice diversion."

"In fact," Roger said, "why don't you both go?"

I'd never seen such a wide smile on my friend Rebecca's face.

A nice couple of hours out of our bathrobes and away from the confines of my house was what the guys had in mind for us. If only they'd known.

Chapter Two
Say, What?

Blue United Taxi dropped us at a condominium complex on Tuscarora Road, a quarter of mile north of the Niagara Falls military airbase. We'd called for the cab, because neither Rebecca with her broken knee, nor I with heavily bandaged ribs, was able to drive.

Amanda Stone lived in a duplex on a corner of the block. When the cab pulled up we saw her waiting just outside the door. Taller than Rebecca's five-foot-ten, with long hair as red as mine (at her age, if had obviously been dyed), at first glance she seemed far younger than my mother had been. She looked from me to my friend, then back at me, as if trying to decide which of us was Anne Goode's daughter. At last, her green eyes settled on me. With an odd smile, she took both of my hands.

"You must be Emlyn," she said. "I can't begin to say how long I've waited to meet you. You look a bit like… Annie."

With her eyes slightly narrowed, Amanda held onto my hands and stared at me long enough that I became somewhat nervous. Could this former friend of my mother actually have been a vampire? Was she studying my neck to find a juicy place to bite? This woman had disappeared years ago. Maybe all this time she'd been lying in a coffin in a dark cellar. And her youthful appearance—vampires didn't age, did they?

All right, I've already admitted I have an overactive imagination.

I peeked at Rebecca from the corner of my eyes. Her forehead creased, she was staring at Amanda Stone with the same intensity as the woman stared at me.

Finally, Amanda released my eyes and my hands. "Please, forgive my ill manners, Emlyn. Introduce me to your friend."

Before I could, Rebecca stuck out her hand. "I… I'm a big Stonemaiden fan. I've collected all your albums."

Amanda chuckled. "In that case, Big Fan, you and my… Um, you and Emlyn come in where we can visit."

A successful writer has to be observant, and over the years I'd learned to be just that. I noticed the way people lean in or away when they converse—this might suggest whether the listener liked or feared what he was hearing. I also paid attention to slips of the tongue. As a result, I noted Amanda's slip. As we followed her into her house, I wondered, *What was that about?*

Seems that while Rebecca had been teaching me the ins and outs of my arcane heritage, she'd learned a bit about observing human behavior from me. I say this, because my friend had also noticed Amanda Stone's slip and quick correction. She'd also seen the way the woman stared at me. Connecting the two dots, she had a theory to explain what she'd observed. As we followed our hostess into her living room, Rebecca grabbed my arm, and whispered, "You look so much like her. She must have thought she was seeing her doppelganger."

I couldn't deny the possibility of seeing a ghost—not after I'd spotted what I'd been certain was the spirit of old Sarah Goode a few times. Still, I had another idea to explain Amanda's behavior.

I began to tell Rebecca that the woman probably reacted as she did because she'd seen much of my mother in my face, but stopped when our hostess turned to us, and asked, "What happened to you. You look like you both took a beating."

I laughed—I could now that the incident was behind us. "A crazy lady thought we were in her way." I mimed swinging a bat.

Amanda, shook her head and *tsked*. "Well, I'm glad it wasn't more serious." She pointed to a sofa, a love seat, an armchair, and a pair of straight-back side chairs, all upholstered in matching floral patterns. "Please make yourselves comfortable, girls. I'll make us some coffee... That is, unless you'd rather have wine."

"Oh, wine. Definitely," I said, and helped Rebecca get settled on one of the straight-back chairs.

The floral motif of the living room didn't end with the furniture. Hanging from the ceiling and resting on tables and in the bay window, were spider plants, bamboo palms, peace lilies, and dracaena.

"You've got quite a garden growing in here," I re-marked when Amanda returned with crystal glasses filled with red wine.

She glanced around, as if seeing the room for the first time. "I like having these in my house. It reminds me how beautiful life can be if only..." Tucking her ankle-length skirt around her legs, she sat on the sofa, and stared through the window at the grass on the common area out back.

She'd just moved here, and this room was fully furnished and decorated. While she sat in silence, I wondered how she'd accomplished this. I'd been living in my converted cottage for years, but still hadn't gotten it to look this finished.

After a few moments, Amanda peered at me, and again seemed to study my face. "Did Annie ever mention me?" she asked.

"Actually, my mother didn't," I said. "I guess that's why receiving your card came as a surprise."

She nodded, and sipped her wine.

When the silence grew as taut as a stretched rubber band, Rebecca poked my arm with her elbow, and whispered, "Say something!"

I mouthed, "What?"

"Say anything. Ask why she disappeared."

"Stop poking me," I whispered, and rested my wine glass on the snack table next to my chair. "Ahem… Uh, Ms. Stone…"

As if I'd called her back from someplace in the past, her eyes focused, and she smiled at me.

"Your note said you knew my mother when she was young," I said. "She never spoke of that time. Would you, uh…"

Amanda Stone's voice took on a dream cast. "We were quite… close in those days, though I wasn't one of those silly girls she hung around with. No. We had a different more… serious relationship. She was my sister—"

"Sister?" What was this woman saying? My mother was an only child.

"Yes. In more ways than one," she said. "We spoke to each other through music. And—"

Uncertain of what she was about to tell me, my stomach quivered.

"—I was two years ahead of her in school, you know? Before she started with those friends of hers, we made wonderful music together." She turned to me. "Annie had a beautiful voice. I thought that she and I... that we could really make hit records."

Is that all? I thought, and released my breath. Obviously, the term *sister* was only a metaphor.

"Why didn't she stay with you?" I asked. "With the music, I mean?"

Amanda Stone shrugged. "Parents didn't approve of the lifestyle." Now, she laughed. "Though looking back at what happened, I can't say those fussy old people were terribly wrong."

This seemed to be moving toward the celebrity gossip Rebecca clearly enjoyed. Nearly bouncing from her seat, she said, "What happened? Is the lifestyle why you disappeared?"

"Your glass is empty," our hostess said. "Let me pour you more wine."

Quickly she moved to her kitchen.

I slapped my friend's wrist. "Now look what you've done. You embarrassed the woman."

Chewing on her lip, Rebecca flipped her braid over her shoulder. "It's been such a big secret. I just wanted—"

"Stop being such a snoop. You're as bad as my cat," I whispered. "It would've come out years ago if she wanted anyone to know."

Amanda Stone came back with the bottle, refilled our glasses, and returned to her corner of the sofa. She nodded to Rebecca. "You asked what happened." To me, she said, "That's part of why I wanted to meet you, Emlyn."

She had our complete attention—Rebecca's, because of the thrill of learning a secret no one else knew; mine, because whatever drove her from the limelight might give me an incredible story to write.

"It was years ago," she began. "Stonemaiden was flying high with hit records and sold out concerts. But the high of it wasn't high enough for Bobby Davis—he was the bass player in the band, and my... partner. To get greater kicks, he arranged wild parties before our concerts, and after-wards..." She pulled a tissue from the sleeve of her tan sweater. "And afterwards..." She took a deep breath, and dabbed the tissue at her heavily made-up eyes. "At one of those parties... I... I was raped."

I gasped. So did Rebecca. "Who... *did* that to you?" my friend asked.

Amanda blew her nose. "I... um, don't know. I was totally stoned at the time. But, after... after... A few weeks later I learned I was pregnant."

"Oh, no!" I didn't know whether Rebeca or I said this.

She gave the deepest sigh I'd ever heard. "So I left the band—disappeared, the trade papers called it—and snuck back here to have my baby. That's when I caught up with Annie."

"What happened to the baby?" Rebecca asked. "The newspapers and magazines never said anything about you giving birth."

Amanda Stone hesitated for what felt like minutes. Then, as if she'd come to a decision, she reached across the coffee table, and took my hand. "*You're* that baby."

Nope. I didn't see *that* coming. I suppose I should have. An observant writer, I should have noticed she never once referred to her friend Anne Goode as my *mother*.

Rebecca shouted, "Oh. My. God!"

Too stunned to speak, I said nothing.

"That's why I've come back here," Amanda continued. "I had to know you, Emlyn... My Emlyn... Also, I think I need your help. I met Grace Linden the other day—what a gossip that woman is, was as a child, too. She told me about you, about how you've helped the police—"

I didn't actually hear any of this. Rebecca had to tell me what Amanda Stone said after she said I was her child. I don't even recall saying, "No! That's a lie! My mother is... My mother... C'mon, Rebecca, we're leaving!"

I half recall that as we hobbled out the door, the woman stood there, saying, "Please, Emlyn. I need you."

Chapter Three
Who Am I?

I had no idea what time Roger came through my front door. It wasn't yet dark, though the sun had begun to dip behind the stand of trees at the far end of my yard. I had been on my patio, stretched out on the chaise lounge since the taxi brought us home. I had no idea how long I'd been laying this way. Once or twice, Elvira had wandered out from the house, and attempted to snuggle next to me. I'd shooed her away.

On that late spring afternoon, I didn't hear birds chirp, didn't feel the gentle breeze float inland from the Niagara River. I wasn't pondering the strange fate that brought me to Amanda Stone's house. That would have required thought, a process for which, at that moment, I didn't have the capacity.

After a while I became slightly aware of voices in the hall near the front door of my house. Roger's voice, Rebecca's.

"What happened?" he asked—his baritone sliced through my haze.

I couldn't hear what Rebecca replied.

He asked, "Where is she?"

The screen slid across the French door. That must have been the sound I heard, because in a moment I saw Roger standing over me.

"Come inside. It's getting chilly." His voice was so soft that it might have been the croon of an owl.

I didn't move, didn't look at him. Why should I? He had spoken to Emlyn *Goqde.* That wasn't me. Not any longer.

His hands slid behind my back. His strong arms lifted me from the chaise. He carried me through the French door, and rested me on my sofa. Then, he knelt at my side and took my hand.

Limping on one crutch, Rebecca came over, and covered me with the gray wool afghan my great-grandmother had knitted a century ago.

"Nothing's really changed," she said. "You're still you."

"Am I?" I whispered, my throat too dry to speak louder.

The cat leaped onto the sofa, and settled between me and the cushions.

Roger scratched between her ears. "Elvira knows who you are."

The cat mewed softly. It was as if she said, *Would I still be here if you weren't you?*

"See," Rebeca said. "Even Elvira knows nothing's changed."

Roger gripped my hand tighter. "Besides, how do know what that woman said was true? She could've been trying to con you."

I rolled onto my side to face the back of the sofa, and pulled the afghan up to my chin. Even the runes Great-Grandma had stitched into it—if she really was my great-grandmother—no longer made sense.

"You need to do something to help her!" Rebecca snarled. "Go talk to Amanda Stone. Grill her till she tells you why she's doing this."

Roger stood. "Good idea. Might be illegal—no evidence Stone's committed a crime. But, right about now I don't care if busting in on her costs me my badge."

The cat's head poked up from the cushions, and she let out an angry *meeeeow!*

"Good idea, Elvira," Rebecca said. "Take Harry with you. He'll know how to beat the truth out of her."

"Just what I plan to do," Roger said. As he walked to the front door, he called over his shoulder, "While Harry and I chat with Stone, brew Emlyn something from the stuff you carry around in your bag. Maybe that'll make her more herself."

§§§

It was quite a while until Roger returned. During the time he was away, Rebecca brewed a pot of tea, made from the "stuff" she had in her oversized shoulder bag. This "stuff" Roger referred to was a mixture of herbs and spices. Rebecca refused to tell me what this mixture contained, no matter how nicely I asked. I was new to this witch-thing, you see, and she feared I might get in a bit of trouble if I attempted to brew one of her concoctions. My friend knew me rather well.

So, as I was saying, Rebecca brewed a pot of her mixture, and through gentle prodding, convinced me to drink some. This remedy had a positive effect. While sipping the second mug of her spice and herbal tea, I began to focus, though I still refused to consider what Amanda Stone had told me. By the third mug, I felt hungry. This was why, when Roger and Harry came in, I was at the kitchen table, munching on a salad Rebecca made me.

"You don't look happy," my friend remarked as the guys dropped onto chairs at my round dinette table.

His lips pinched, Harry shook his head.

"Couldn't get that bird to sing?" Rebecca said.

Bird? Sing? Clearly, my friend had been watching too many crime films since she'd been dating Harry.

My appetite evaporated as quickly as water left in a tropical sun. I pushed away my plate "You were gone a long time? Did my... Did *Amanda* say anything?"

Roger stared out the window at the woods on the other side of River Road. "She couldn't," he said.

"Why not?" Rebecca demanded.

With a sigh, Harry answered, "When we got to her house, Amanda Stone was dead."

"That's what took so long," Roger added. "Had to call it in, then wait for the Crime Scene Unit." A small smile on his lips, he looked at Harry. "Good thing you were with me, Chief. Saved me a lot of explaining about why I was there."

Shock in her voice, Rebeca asked, "What happened?"

Roger peeked at me, as if he were uncertain whether I'd regained enough strength to hear the details.

"I don't think so, Detective," Harry shook his head, and leaned back in his chair. "This is a police matter."

"I *have* to know," I said.

I refused to believe what Amanda Stone had told me. Still, if it were true... I gulped back tears, and silently prayed, *Fiery god of the sun, bringer of life, lend me strength that I might bear what lies ahead.*

With a deep breath, I repeated, "I have to know."

Elvira had been lapping the milk in her bowl. When Roger hesitated, she raised her head, and fixed him with a stare. Her pink eyes seemed to send the message, *Better tell Emlyn. She knows a spell that'll have you talking in falsetto.*

As if he'd understood my cat, Roger cleared his throat. "Actually, Chief, she's a witness—they both are. Plus, they've helped us in the past."

Harry thought about this for a minute, then clicked his tongue. "All right. If you all need to know."

Apparently satisfied, the cat parked herself beneath the table.

"When we got to Tuscarora Road," Roger said, "we found the bay window at the side of Stone's house broken—"

"From the outside," Harry added.

Roger looked at him.

"If you're gonna tell it, Detective, you've got to be exact."

"Okay, then. The window was broken from the outside. We went around back, looked in, and saw the Stone woman sprawled on the floor in the middle of her living room."

"Yes," Harry said. "And we could make out a pistol on the floor near her hand."

"So we used a rock to break through the glass door to get in. She'd been shot, all right—"

"A single bullet, in her left temple. Through-and-through."

Roger nodded. "The weapon was a .22 caliber Berretta. Crime Scene said at first glance it matched the wound. Won't know for sure till after the autopsy."

"Could she have killed herself?" Rebecca asked.

It was Harry that answered. "Window broken like someone got in that way? Doubtful."

"When you two were with her," Roger said, "did you notice if she was right- or left-handed?"

I thought about that. "Right-handed... I think." I blinked a few times, trying to bring back the memory, then said, "Yes. She held the bottle in her right hand when she poured wine into our glasses, so she has... had to be right-handed."

"That sort of settles it, then. Even if *she* had the gun, couldn't be that the killer turned on her."

"It's a burglary gone bad," Harry said. "And don't forget the place looked like it had been ransacked." He pulled his cellphone from his jacket pocket. "Got a picture of the place." He handed me his phone. "Took this after the body was removed."

The photo showed Amanda's living room. Chairs overturned, cabinets open, knick-knacks on the floor as if they'd been tossed over someone's shoulder while he dug for what he sought.

Roger took the phone from me, and gave it back to his boss. "But, what about her front door?" he said. "It wasn't locked. Could she have known our perp? Let him in, and the killer wanted to make it look like something else? And, there was that note."

"Note?" I asked.

"Yeah," Roger said. "It was in her kitchen sink. Mostly burnt."

My appetite began to come back. I lifted my fork, and took a bite of my salad. While chewing, I asked, "What did the note say?"

Roger reached into the back pocket of his slacks, and pulled out his notepad. "Wasn't much of it left." He flipped up a page. "What we could make out was, '…couldn't hide forever… it's mine.'" He closed his pad and looked over at Harry.

"That's one more thing that tells me she knew who killed her."

Harry pulled at his lower lip and stared up at the ceiling. "The more we talk, the more I'm coming around to that."

Rebecca had been putting up a pot of coffee while the guys described what they'd found. Carrying the pot and mugs to the dinette table, she asked," But, you should be able to find whoever did this? I mean, he left his gun behind."

Harry shook his head. "Whoever killed Stone was careful. The number on the gun was filed off. Plus, the killer either used gloves or wiped his prints. Crime Scene didn't find any in their first test. If I know those guys, they'll keep trying, though— even dust the remaining bullets."

As Roger and Harry finished describing the scene of Amanda Stone's murder, moisture filled my eyes. Roger noticed my tears—this man loved me enough to notice every nuance.

"I knew this would upset you." He looked over at Rebecca, who was standing near the stove. "We shouldn't have told you all this."

I wiped my eyes on my sleeve. "No, it's not that."

"What, then?"

"I think whoever killed Amanda doesn't want me to find out if... I am who I always thought I was."

Roger lifted my long red hair, and kissed my neck. "Don't worry about this. It's far too early to assign a motive for the killing."

"That's right," Harry agreed. "And if we're gonna find that motive, we've got work to do. So, let's get busy, Detective."

Roger rubbed my cheek. "See you later."

Harry blew a kiss to Rebecca. As they walked to the door, he said, "You two, behave yourselves. You hear me? No mixing into this case."

Roger laughed. "These two? You must be kidding, Chief." He looked down at my cat. "Elvira, I'm depending on you to see they stay out of trouble."

I swear, that plus-size albino suck-up nodded.

Chapter Four
If Anyone Would Know

As soon as I heard Roger's Trailblazer back out of my driveway, I pushed myself up from the chair (my ribs heavily bandaged, I couldn't rise gracefully). At the kitchen counter, I grabbed my purse.

"Come on," I said to Rebecca.

Leaning on her crutch, she scratched her chin. "Come on where?"

"To Amanda Stone's house, of course. There has to be something the cops missed."

"It's a crime scene. It's probably roped-off. If we go in, we'll get arrested."

I grumbled. "If you're afraid of something like that, I'll go alone."

I took a few slow steps, then stopped. My pink-eyed fur-ball was parked in the doorway.

"Get out of my way, animal," I snarled.

The cat hissed at me. I'm certain she'd said, *Who are you calling an animal?*

I refused to be deterred. "I said, move over!"

Elvira shook her head.

I stamped my foot. "What are you doing, cat?"

Behind me, Rebecca laughed. When I turned my head to her, she said, "Roger told Elvira to keep you from getting in trouble."

I tried to lean down and shove my cat aside, then abruptly stood up, holding my ribs.

Still laughing, Rebecca said, "That's the other reason we can't go anywhere."

"What is?"

"You're not able to drive, and neither am I. And you can't call a cab, because I saw Roger pocket your wallet." She took the purse from my hand, and put it back on the counter. "That's why the guys didn't worry about leaving us here. So, come into the living room, and pour us some wine."

"I can't just waste the evening drinking," I whined. "I have to do something. I feel as though my life's been dropped on its head. Did Amanda lie? If she didn't, after all these years, why'd she show up now? I need to know."

She took my arm, and thumbed away the tears that formed. "I know. And I want to help you. But this time we'll have to figure it out here." She smiled at me. "Armchair detectives, like the kind you always read about. Do that, and maybe we won't almost get killed again."

I sniffed. "Okay, you win. I'll get the wine. You get Sarah's book from my desk.

See if she wrote something that might get my brain working."

I might have been wrong, but I thought I heard my cat sigh with relief.

§§§

Two glasses of a good chardonnay I'd purchased last summer during a tasting at Arrowhead Spring Vineyard did little to calm the quivering in my chest. Each sip recalled the wine we'd had in Amanda Stone's living room that afternoon. Pressed in a corner of my sofa with Elvira snuggled tight at my side, I stared into the darkness on the other side of the French door.

Fortunately, Rebecca was able to focus. In the over-stuffed chair next to my bookcases, she carefully turned the brittle pages of Sarah Goode's *Book of Shadows*.

"Here's something that could make you feel a little better." She looked up from the old calf-bound book. "Sandalwood chips, red carnation petals, and rosemary leaves, crushed in a green glass jar that's then filled with olive oil. Sarah wrote that she used this to ease the anxiety of a farmer named Henry Clark during an extended dry period."

Elvira sat up, and nodded—at least, it looked like she did.

I sighed. "Did it work?"

Rebecca glanced down, turned the page, then turned back to the page she'd been reading. "It doesn't say. Apparently Sarah got hanged a few days after she wrote this entry."

"Great," I said, while refilling my glass. "Rub that tincture all over my body, and whoever killed Amanda will smell me as soon as he turns onto River Road. Then, he'll know exactly what house to break into next, and come here and hang *me*."

Rebecca closed the book. With her head still down, she raised her eyes. "I'm *trying* to help."

I closed *my* eyes and took a breath. "I know. I'm sorry."

"Look, Emlyn, Amanda Stone probably lied when she claimed to be your mother. I mean, what proof did she have?"

"I don't know…" I groaned. "And now that she's dead I'll never know."

"Well, maybe…" My friend sat up straight in her chair. As if petting a cat, she began to stroke her long braid. This was what she would do when concentrating. After a minute, she said, "Um, there could be a way to tell." She lifted her shoulder bag from the floor next to her chair, and dug into it for her cellphone. "They'll be able to get Amanda Stone's DNA, and it's a simple thing to give them yours for comparison."

I shook my head. "The lab's constantly overloaded—Roger once told me that. It'll take months before they can run DNA tests. That means it'll be months before I'm able to sleep again."

"Well, they can at least check her blood type. That won't take long. And Memorial Hospital already has yours. Checking that will at least be a clue."

At last, a glimmer of light. Blood matching wouldn't be what lawyers call "dispositive" of a relationship (I'd come across that term while researching a story), but if our blood types didn't match, it would at least be some indication that Amanda had lied.

Elvira leaned over and looked up at me. She purred, because, for the first time in hours I was smiling.

Immediately Rebecca punched Harry's number into her phone.

After half a bottle of Chardonnay, I hoped I'd be able to sleep. At least for that one night.

§§§

If I were smart, I would have remained in bed, sleeping the next day away. Had I, I would have been able to hold onto the hope a blood test would prove Amanda Stone lied. I didn't stay in bed, because when sunlight broke through my window the next morning, I smelled coffee. Then I heard Roger and Rebecca talking downstairs.

"Blood results came back this morning," Roger said.

I didn't hear what Rebecca said. She was speaking softly. Still, I sensed an urgency in her voice. This urgency whispered a warning in my ear. Hope deafened me to that inner whisper.

Forgetting my sore ribs, I jumped from my bed, threw on my robe, and nearly tripped over Elvira as I came through the bedroom door. She let out a screech. Then, I heard limping feet moving from my living room to the kitchen. Apparently, that feline rat-fink was serving as an early warning system. But, warning about what?

Moving hesitantly now, I went downstairs.

In the kitchen, Roger was at the window. Dressed in jeans and a corduroy jacket, he watched the cars carrying people to work in Buffalo or Niagara Falls. River Road connected the two cities.

Wearing her bathrobe and slippers, with a crutch under one arm, Rebecca was topping off a mug of coffee with Irish whiskey. She tried to hide the bottle behind her back when I came through the door.

Without turning around, Roger said, "Might as well tell her now as later."

Having a reasonable idea of what I was about to hear, I steadied myself by leaning against the white Formica counter.

"*You* brought the results, you tell her," Rebecca said.

He sighed, and took the coffee mug from the dinette table. Handing it to me, he said, "Amanda Stone's blood is B-negative. Kind of rare—only five percent of people have it."

"I'm B-negative," I muttered.

Elvira had maneuvered her large body so that she now sat at my feet. Bless that animal, it was as if she intended to be a cushion if I fainted. That proved to be unnecessary. Roger had me in his arms, transferring his strength to me.

"It's only suggestive," he said.

"That's right," Rebecca quickly agreed. "Didn't Amanda suggest she was you mother's sister? If she was, her blood type could run in your family."

I latched onto the idea. "That's right. My mother also had that type. I remember— she had a card from the Red Cross from a time she donated blood."

"See?" Roger said. "So, this doesn't prove anything."

"Still," I wondered aloud, "why didn't Mom ever tell me she had a sister?"

"Families can be strange," Rebecca said. "Think about mine. I was sixteen when I found out by accident I was adopted."

Roger kissed my forehead. "I guess that's one of those things we'll need to find out." Releasing me, as he headed for the door, he said, "In fact, I'm gonna start finding out right now."

To myself, I said, "So am I."

Rebecca caught her breath.

Elvira *meowed.* I'm pretty sure my cat had said, *Uh-oh.*

Chapter Five
Sources

The current condition Rebecca and I were in prevented an excursion to the Rochester home in which Doris Bishop, my second-cousin on my mother's side had been placed. Even had I been able to undertake that drive, the only family member who might have traced my mother's branch on our family tree hadn't had a lucid moment in the past six months. As a result, phoning her would also be pointless. This left only one thing. By the time Rebecca came into my living room, I was settled on the sofa with that *one thing* open on my lap, and a magnifying glass in my hand.

"Now, isn't this better than chasing after crazy people who want to kill us?" she said. Leaning her crutches against the arm of the sofa, she eased down next to me. "What are you looking at?"

Focused on an entry my ancient relative had made on May 6, 1692, I didn't respond.

"Tell me," Rebecca said.

When I still didn't answer, she moved so close she was almost on my lap.

It was this entry that held me so engrossed I hardly felt her:

Restless have I grown these past days. This hovel in which I dwell is as much a cell as that into which I fear I shall soon be cast. Evil times are these when Satan walks among us unseen. Who is this Satan that works his evil in the names of good women? This must I learn or perish. Three parts cinquefoil, three parts chicory root, and one part clove ground together on this Wednesday night will make he that is unseen be seen. Yet watched so closely am I that I dare not use my herbs to know that mocking face. So must I go out into this Salem Town that I might seek him out.

Rebecca had clearly read this passage along with me, and knew what I had in mind. Immediately, my friend's face turned pale. She snatched Sarah Goode's *Book of Shadows* from my hand, and slid to the other side of the sofa.

My cat had been dozing on my overstuffed chair. Now, her head popped up. Yawning, she gazed around.

"It's entirely reasonable," I said, more to myself than to my friend.

"It's not," Rebecca insisted.

I smiled at her. "We'd just be talking to people."

Her full lips pinched into a thin, straight line.

"And, we'd be doing it without using witchcraft," I continued. "How much trouble could we get into?"

Clutching the book to her chest, my friend shook her head, which caused her long braid to flop from one shoulder to the other.

I pointed to the book. "But, Sarah, wrote—"

My cat nodded.

"Elvira, don't encourage this crazy person!" Rebecca shouted.

"Oh, come on. You don't want to just sit here and do nothing, do you?"

"Nothing is just what we oughta do. We're safe in your nice comfortable house. We have food. We have wine. We've got boyfriends who are cops, and want us to stay safe and snug while *they* find out who killed Amanda Stone. What else do we need?"

"Even if they catch the culprit, they won't find out if Amanda was really my mother. That's what *I* need." Leaning on the coffee table, I pushed myself up, and stood in front of Rebecca with my hands on my hips. "Get dressed."

She gripped the arm of the sofa. "Where are you going? Have you forgotten we're in no condition to drive and we have no money for a taxi?"

I laughed. "I just remembered that I know someone who drives a cab."

Elvira's tongue flitted across her cat-lips. I'm sure she was thinking, *Ooh, this is gonna be fun.*

§§§

The cab from Blue United Taxi pulled into my driveway and honked. I opened my door and waved—a universal signal that meant, *I'll be another minute.*

Five minutes after my boyfriend had left my house, I was on the phone making plans to have lunch with Harriet Sovronsky. Harriet's daughter had been in high school with my mother, so she'd know if Mom had a sister.

Dressed in a linen maroon vest over a similarly colored long-sleeve pullover, Rebecca hung onto her crutches with one hand while she shrugged her ten-gallon bag onto her shoulder.

"Why can't you let Roger talk to her?" she complained.

"He's a cop," I said. "People will talk to me more easily than they would to him." Checking my red hair in the hall mirror, I thought, *Especially Harriet. After what happened at Mom's reunion, she gets nervous just being near a cop.*

Rebecca broke into my thought. "I still don't think this is a good idea."

I opened the door, and stepped outside. "Stay here, then. I can talk to Harriet by myself."

"Uh-uh," she said. "Left on your own, you'll either get arrested or killed."

The leg of her floral pants had been cut so it would fit over her cast. The material flopped in the breeze when she followed me outside.

When we were settled in the back seat of the cab, I saw a row of very white teeth smiling at us in the rearview mirror.

"Looks like you're doin' better, Emlyn. Ribs healin' fine?" the driver said.

I laughed. "I'm much better, Miguel. Thanks."

At the risk of repeating myself, Niagara Falls was more like a small town than a city. Those of us who'd grown up here knew each other—sometimes uncom-fortably so. I'd gone to high school with Miguel Riviera's older sister, and once was nearly expelled with her when we were caught breaking into the boys locker room during a school dance.

"Where to?" he asked.

"Michael's on Pine Avenue.

"Know the place," he said as he backed out of my driveway. "My mother swears by their marinara sauce. Hey, remind me to buy 'er a quart when I drop y'off."

I'd suggested meeting at Michael's, because Harriet Sovronsky lives just a few blocks away on Ferry Street and could easily walk there. Okay, I had another reason. Now that I had a mission, I was hungry and had a craving for one of Michael's calzones. They fried this treat, and served it with a marinara dipping sauce.

Miguel parked in the lot behind the restaurant so he could buy the quart of sauce for his mother. When we came through the back door, I stopped, looked around, and spotted Harriet at a table by the front window. Waving away Eva who approached us with a handful of menus and a smile, we joined her.

Only about five-two, Harriet had a round face and rosy cheeks, even in the summer. Her grandmotherly appearance always reminded me of the picture of Mrs. Claus in a book I'd had as a child. In all the years I'd known this woman, I couldn't recall her looking other than like this.

"I'm glad to see you girls out and about," she said when Rebecca and I at sat down at the table.

"Thank you for the flowers and all the candy while we were in the hospital," I said.

Rebecca leaned over and pecked a kiss on Harriet's cheek.

A volunteer at Memorial, she had visited Rebecca and me several times each day during the week we'd been hospitalized. In part, this was because she'd known me since my childhood. The other part was a dark secret Rebecca and I had kept—a secret involving a girl who was dead, and then was dead again.

When our lunch was brought to the table, I prepared to raise the subject that had brought us here. I didn't get a chance to, though. Just as I opened my mouth, I heard the window rattle as if it had been smacked by a gale wind. But, the day was calm. Startled, I glanced up.

On the other side of the glass, I saw Roger's grinning face. He wagged his index finger at me.

"Damn!" I groused.

Less than a minute later, Michael's front door opened, and Roger ambled to our table. "Got room for two more?" he said.

"Two?" Rebecca asked.

He stood aside. The man was so tall and broad across the chest, neither my friend nor I had noticed the stumpy woman with short gray hair standing behind him. This was Grace Linden.

"Damn, damn!" I muttered.

Without an invitation, Roger pulled out a chair for Grace, and dropped onto the other empty seat. Through what I can only describe as a wicked smile, he said, "I'm glad to see you two resting comfortably at home, and letting *me* do the investigating."

I gulped. When my guy pushed the sarcasm button, he pushed it hard.

"I, um… we were bored, and, uh… my good friend Harriet was free for lunch…"

I looked across the table at Rebecca, my eyes begging her for help. My supposed friend turned to the window.

"Oh," she said. "Look at that old car parked across the street. It's a Model-A, I think."

Had she been sitting closer, I would have punched her.

Grace snickered, and hung the plastic supermarket bag she always carried on the back of her chair. The town rumor-monger, this woman kept a bag that people said contained gossip about everyone she knew—and she knew practically everyone in town.

Still looking at me, Roger said, "Since you've been kind enough to make Harriet available, mind if I ask her a few questions?"

I saw the elderly woman shudder. Not knowing what information Roger wanted, she must have feared he intended to dig into that dark secret I mentioned. This was the reason I'd wanted to talk to her myself. Now that Roger had broken in on us, I could only hope I'd be able to metaphorically elbow him aside and ask the only question I needed answered.

"You knew my mother a long time," I said before Roger had a chance to speak. "Is it possible she had, um… a relative I didn't know about?"

It was Grace Linden that answered. "You mean 'Manda Stone?" Again she snickered. "Your other mother?"

I glared at her.

"How do you know about that?" Roger asked.

Gossip-Grace patted her hair. With a look of innocence, she replied, "I was down to Frankie's Donuts for breakfast this mornin' when that lawyer, Howard Kline, come in to get coffee. He told me. By now, everyone in town knows."

"I bet they do," Rebecca hissed. "And I just bet I know who told everyone." She raised a crutch, as if she were ready to beat Grace with it."

Roger grabbed her hand. To Grace, he said, "Did Kline tell you how he knew that?"

"Well…" She looked down at the table, and whispered, "I don't think I should say. He told me in confidence."

Now, Harriet appeared ready to hit the woman.

"You'll tell me, Grace, right now!" Roger demanded. "Or, I'll give you a ride to precinct, and you'll tell me there."

"Okay, okay." She leaned away from him. "Ya don't hafta get mean about it."

"I'm waiting," Roger said.

"Oh, all right. Amanda Stone went to Howard to have her Will done. Said she wanted to see to the needs of 'er daughter." Glaring at Roger, she stood. "Got what ya wanted from me now? Then I'm leavin', and you can't stop me."

She stomped out of Michael's rubbing her wrist. If I were to bet on it, I'd have laid odds that by evening half of Niagara Falls would be told Roger had *beaten* the information out of her.

When the door swished closed behind Grace Linden, Harriet remarked, "I never liked her. Rotten. Was, even when she was a girl."

To that, Rebecca added, "Definitely a witch that should've been lynched in Salem."

Roger glanced at Rebecca then at me, perhaps wondering whether my distant relative had been that kind of witch. After a moment, he said, "Stone wanted to look out for her daughter, huh? I know where my next stop is, and guess who's coming with me."

"I can't." I said. "I want to talk to Harriet about—"

The man fixed a wide grin at me. "Yeah? Well, things are tough all over."

Chapter Six
The Seneca Building

The Seneca Nation had turned the old Niagara Falls Convention Center into a state-of-the-art casino and hotel. It had floors of slot machines with jackpot lights and bells going off several times an hour, and blackjack, poker, and craps for the more dedicated gamblers. I'm not one of those, haven't been since the time God sent me a message. That happened one evening when my ex-husband and I joined neighbors at a friendly game of poker. As I recall, I held the nine of diamonds and the nine of spades, dropped three cards, and drew the other two nines. Four of a kind, a sure winning hand, right? Uh-uh. Not when a woman sitting across from me had a royal flush. Thank you, God. Message received. Since that time, when I went to the casino it was to enjoy one of its restaurants, or a show. I mention this, because while Roger drove us to Howard Kline's office, an advertisement on the radio said Stonemaiden would be performing at the Seneca Niagara Casino two nights that week. A coincidence? Roger had taught me not to believe in those.

He looked over at me when we heard that ad. "Stone's old band is in the Falls at the same time she was killed? I'm thinking there are more people I need to talk to."

From the back seat, Rebecca said, "Great. Let's get tickets for one of their shows." Once again, she was the teenage rock fan. "You know, just to hear if they still sound like their records."

"This isn't play time," Roger said.

"Well… we can talk to the band *after* the concert."

"Can't wait that long. Gotta find them, talk to 'em today if I can."

"Not without me," I said.

"Oh, me, too," Rebecca said.

His eyes on the road, the man ignored us both.

Across from the casino, straddling Fourth Street and Rainbow Boulevard, stood a five story building. Included with the land given to the Seneca Nation, this building housed the casino offices. It also housed the offices of Howard Kline, Esq.

Not overly large, the reception area of Kline's third-floor offices was paneled in dark-stained oak. In front of the reception desk, a three-seat brown leather couch and two matching armchairs surrounded a polished mahogany table, on which were several issues of the *Law Journal*.

While Rebecca sat in one of the armchairs, Roger draped his arm around my waist, and steered me to the middle-aged, dark-haired receptionist.

"We need to see Mr. Kline about one of his clients," he said.

The woman stopped typing. "Mr. Kline is rather busy today. Do you have an appointment, Mr.—" She examined us, then dropped her gaze to an appointment book on her desk.

Roger handed her his business card, and showed her his badge. "That's *Detective* Frey. And it's urgent that we seem him now."

The authority in his voice all but caused the woman to jump to attention. Immediately, she picked up her phone and pushed the intercom button.

"A policeman is here to see you, Mr. Kline. He says it's important." After a moment, she looked up at us. "He's just finishing with some people. He'll be able to see you in a few minutes."

Before we had a chance to take seats, the door next to the receptionist's desk opened, and five men came through. As two of them shook hands, one said, "I'm sorry there's not much more I can tell you."

Dressed in a black Perry Ellis suit with a red and white power tie, Howard Kline had a long straight nose, and his slicked-back, black hair was perfectly parted two inches left of center. I recognized him by sight and by voice. Several years earlier, I sat on a jury in a criminal trial. He was the defense attorney.

"There'll be a formal reading of Ms. Stone's Will after her memorial service a week from Thursday," Kline continued. "As I said, that's in accordance with her instructions."

This was when things got interesting.

Almost springing from her chair, Rebecca called. "It's Bobby Davis!" She pointed to one of the men. "You're… Bobby…"

I expected that any moment she would tear off her clothes and jump on him.

Davis appeared to be about five-foot ten, two inches shorter than Amanda Stone had been. His gaunt face, stained with each of his sixty-nine years, was almost as gray as his hair. He had on a white and black checked flannel shirt, the sleeves rolled up far enough to expose a rose tattoo on his forearm.

Too many drinks, drugs, or just too much life? I wondered, thinking how I might portray him as a character in one of my stories.

Roger stepped up to the group of men, and showed his badge. Quickly, he introduced Rebecca and me, then said, "I'm glad to find you all together. Can we step into your office, Mr. Kline? I suspect each of you has some information I need in my Amanda Stone case."

Appearing a bit uncertain, Kline glanced at his receptionist.

"You have a meeting on the Reedy matter in a half hour," she said.

"Can we do this another time, Detective?" Kline asked. "I'd like to prepare for my next meeting.

Roger stared the man down. "I'm afraid I have to insist. If everyone cooperates, I'm sure this won't take too long."

Kline made a single, sharp nod. "All right, then. And I'm sure you won't mind if I have my secretary sit in and take notes."

The lawyer led us to a large room with wide windows overlooking Rainbow Boulevard. Once we were seated around the conference table, Roger said, "It seems everyone here is interested in my victim's Will." He gave a brief smile in my direction. "What say, we start with that?"

How could I not love this man? Even when he worked a case, he looked out for me.

Without hesitation, Kline responded, "I'm sure you'll understand, Detective—" He glanced down at Roger's card. "—Frey. As I told these gentlemen, that's confidential."

"Really?" Roger tilted his head. "That's not what Grace Linden led me to believe."

The lawyer's neck grew red, then the flush rose to his cheeks.

Without skipping a beat, Roger added, "Besides, sitting with us—" He gestured toward me. "—is Emlyn Goode. As I understand it, in the Will she's Stone's sole heir.

Kline still hesitated.

"Of course," Roger said, "I could get a subpoena. But, that would tie us up here three or four hours while we wait for it."

With a sigh, Kline said to his secretary. "Janet, please bring me the Stone file."

My stomach quaked. Was I coming closer to an answer?

"I suppose it doesn't make a difference if we do this now or later," Kline said. "While Ms. Goode isn't the sole heir, everyone mentioned in her Will is in this room."

The two minute wait for the file felt like an eternity. Okay, I know I had no idea what eternity felt like, but in that two minutes I came close to learning. From the seat next to mine, Rebecca reached over and gripped my hand. She seemed to be as nervous as I.

When, at last, the file was placed before Kline, he said, "This is a rather simple document, actually. A few small bequests— Mr. Davis, to you she left her collection of guitars. She says that's in memory of the years you made music together."

The lawyer's expression was totally deadpan, so I couldn't tell if he caught the *double entendre*.

"This collection includes…" he went on. "How did she put it?" He looked down at the file. "Ah, yes. Her vintage Les Paul guitar. To you, Mr. Simms—" Kline turned to Jeffrey Simms, the band's drummer. "— and to you, Mr. Louellen—" Now, he turned and nodded to Rick Louellen, Stonemaiden's lead guitarist. "—she left twenty thousand dollars each, with the hope you don't waste it on drugs and women."

The older man at the far end of the table began to fidget. Mussed white hair, jowls, and deep lines around his eyes and down his cheeks, he looked to be pushing eighty. From the earlier introductions, I knew this was Eric Riley, the band's manager.

Kline acknowledged him with a nod. "To you, Mr. Riley, Ms. Stone left a thousand dollars, and—she told me to read this exactly—I'm to tell you she said, 'thanks for the ride'."

The manager's forehead creased into a deep frown, as if he were exceedingly aggravated about the pittance his former client had left him.

When Kline shifted his gaze to me, I felt Rebecca's grip tighten on my hand. "The rest, residue, and remainder of Ms. Stone's estate, is left to Emlyn Goode," he said. "This includes some mutual funds and her house on Tuscarora Road. Oh, and there's this."

He removed a key from the file, and handed it to me. That done, he sat back.

Nervously, Eric Riley looked to Bobby Davis, then to Simms, then Rick Louellen. It was Louellen that asked, "That's all? That's everything?"

"That's it," Kline said.

Simms leaned so far forward, his greasy, long hair fell over his face. "There wasn't a—"

Davis grabbed his arm, and shook his head.

"As I said, that's everything." Kline looked across the table. "Are we finished here, Detective?"

Roger, who'd been listening and watching intently throughout the Will reading, grinned. "Oh, no. We're just getting started."

Groans came from around the table. Howard Kline's was the loudest.

Pulling his pad and a pen from his jacket pocket, Roger said, "Nothing in Stone's Will as you read it says Emlyn Goode is her daughter. Yet you told Grace Linden she is."

As before, the mention of Kline's indiscretion with Gossip-Grace brought a flush to his cheeks. Clearing his throat, he said, "My client asked for advice on how to be certain this document couldn't be challenged. I gave her a list of family members who might be successful in challenging it. Then she said, 'That's good. I only have one living relative—my daughter, Emlyn'." The lawyer thought for a moment. "Funny thing about that. She didn't want Ms. Goode mentioned as her daughter in her Will. Still, for protection—hers as well as mine—I had her sign an affidavit to that effect."

He shuffled through the file, took out a single page, and held it out.

Roger made a note, then asked, "Did you know Amanda Stone before she moved to Niagara Falls?"

Kline shook his head. "She said she came to me because she read a newspaper report about the Munroe estate. That's a matter I'm handling."

What I mentioned earlier about Niagara Falls being like a small town? Who got what from the Munroe estate was part of what landed me and Rebecca in the hospital.

"One more question," Roger said. "You gave Emlyn a key. Do you know what it's to?"

"A safe deposit box, I presume. My client gave me the key, but told me nothing about it."

After making another note, Roger asked, "I don't suppose you know what's in that box?"

Kline shrugged. "No idea."

"Thanks for your time, then. You and your secretary can go." Waving his hand around the room, he said, "I have just a few questions for these gentlemen."

Halfway to his feet, the attorney abruptly sat down. "In that case, Detective, I'd better stay. These people have just signed on as my clients."

"Is that so?" Roger looked doubtful.

Each member of the band and the manager nodded in turn.

"Okay, then, you can stay." Glancing around at the band members, Roger said, "My victim moved up here a few weeks ago. But, of course, you knew that, didn't you?"

Simms and Louellen looked at Davis, who glanced in the direction of Riley.

Patting his jacket pocket, the manager said, "None of us had any idea."

The others answered, "Didn't know." "Uh-uh." "Never heard 'bout it."

"Strange, don't you think? Stone moved here, and within a few weeks you're here to perform at the casino. And no sooner do you arrive than she's dead." Roger shook his head at the incredulity of such a thought.

"Whaddaya want me to say," Davis answered. "Eric here booked the gig. I didn't know where the hell 'Manda was. Ain't seen 'er in what? Thirty years? But I'll tell ya this. I loved that crazy lady." His voice broke, and he rubbed his sleeve across his eyes. "Love 'er still, even now she's dead. No way I'd ever…" He sniffed and turned toward the windows.

If this was an act, it was a good one. I made a mental note to write a story built on relationships that survive decades of turmoil.

Again, Roger tilted his head. Clearly, he didn't buy Davis's performance. He pressed the man with additional questions, but couldn't move him off his original statement.

Rick Louellen was questioned next. Dressed in jeans and a stained acid rock t-shirt, he was the tallest of the group. A single glance at his hands told me he used them on more than his guitar. His knuckles were bruised, and he had a bandage on his right wrist.

"I suppose you also loved Amanda Stone?" Roger said.

"Nah. Wouldn't go near 'er. Lady was a total nutcase."

"Didn't like her much, huh?"

Louellen didn't answer.

"Must've ticked you off thoroughly when she dis-appeared on the band."

"Yeah, I sure hated 'er for that."

"Enough to kill her?"

"Hey!" The man sounded outraged. "I never killed no one."

"Wanna tell me where you got those bruises?"

Howard Kline laid a hand on Louellen's arm, and shook his head. "That happened in a bar fight last night, Detective. There's probably police record on it."

Jeff Simms had a bandage on the bridge of his nose and a black eye. When questioned about those injuries, he replied, "I was just makin' sure my friend, Rick, didn't get the worst of it in that fight."

After I'd received the card from Amanda, I Googled Stonemaiden. A few websites called the band 'a bunch of brawlers'. Seeing them thirty years later, it struck me that, save for the wrinkles and gray hair, not much had changed.

Finally, it was Eric Riley's turn, though I didn't see the point in questioning him. I mean, at his age?

Apparently, Roger didn't engage in ageism when a murder was involved. He pushed Riley hard, yet the man remained calm. Chewing on an unlit cigar, he said, "Sure I was angry at her for up and disappearing the way she did. Cost me a bundle in commissions. But, Stonemaiden still got work. And if their performances didn't pay what they used to, so what? I was still making enough to keep me in imported cigars the few years I've got left."

An hour and a quarter had gotten Roger no closer to learning who killed Amanda Stone. And though I had inherited some money, I felt no satisfaction. A woman who said I was really her daughter had asked for my help, but I'd denied her. Worse, lost in a haze of self-pity, I'd cursed the day she entered my life. Now she'd been killed. I couldn't live with that.

We left Kline's conference room. Just as the secretary closed the door, I heard Riley say, "You guys go rehearse—you need it."

"Where you goin'?" Simms asked.

"Next door. Wanna see the casino's booker."

Davis asked, "The gig's still on?"

"That's what I wanna find out," Riley said.

I see how much Bobby Davis misses the woman he loved, I thought.

Chapter Seven
The Key

The entire ride home in Roger's Trailblazer, Rebecca giggled. "My friend is rich!" she said. "I can't believe it. You have to tell me what kind of spell you cast to do that."

"I didn't do anything," I muttered. "Not a single thing."

"Maybe it was a stray thought you had."

I didn't answer.

"I've told you to be careful about what you think. Stray thoughts sometimes float out and make things happen." She leaned from the back seat, and rubbed my shoulder. "This time something good."

My spirits should have been as light as my friend's. Yes, I had most of what Amanda left behind. But, she'd left that to her *daughter*.

As we slowed for the light at Williams Road, I moaned, "The money and the house aren't mine. *Anne Goode* was my mother." As if it were a mantra, over and over I softly repeated, "Anne Goode was my mother."

Roger, who'd been lost in thought since we left Fourth Street, took my hand.

"Chances are Stone lied about being your mother. You heard what that lawyer said."

"What did he say?"

"The woman was just looking for a way to keep what she had out of someone else's hands. She didn't come up with the idea of a daughter until Kline put it in her head."

This stopped my muttering. I turned in my seat to look at him. "Whose hands?"

His eyes straight ahead, he said, "That's what I've been trying to figure out."

Obviously, he kept trying to figure it out the rest of the way to my house. He didn't utter another word until he pulled into my driveway. Even then, he said only, "Woody's here."

From the time he was a Marine Colonel during Desert Storm, Harry Woodward's men referred to him as Woody. In no sense a slur, the nickname indicated the respect they had for him. In war, this stalwart officer would never cut and run, nor would he leave a soldier behind. Roger knew this of Harry. He'd served under him in Iraq. More than once Roger had spoken to me of a time Woody pulled him out of danger during that war.

As soon as Roger turned off the ignition, Harry climbed from his Buick Enclave. A few long strides brought him to the driver's-side window, where he tapped on the SUV's roof.

Roger rolled down the window.

"Looks like you've been busy." Harry leaned down, and looked through the window first at me in the passenger seat, then at Rebecca in back. With a half-smile that was little more than a twitch of his lips, he said, "You arrest these two criminals for interfering with police business again?"

Rebecca laughed; I rolled my eyes.

"Thought about it, Chief," Roger replied. "But they actually turned out to be rather helpful."

Harry opened the back door to help Rebecca get out. While he did, he said, "As I recall, Detective, I've spoken to you about keeping civilians out of your investigations."

"These two?" Roger poked my arm. "You must be kidding."

Rubbing his short, military-cut hair, Harry said, "You've got a point there. Want to tell me what you learned?"

"How about we do it over dinner? I'm hungry enough to eat a whole cow by myself—including the hooves."

Because I was able to hold onto the hope Roger had been correct when he told me Amanda invented the story about being my mother, I now also felt hungry enough to eat a cow. Well, perhaps not a cow, but maybe a good-sized calf. The problem was, I had nothing in the house but salad makings. I pointed this out to the guys.

"Not to worry," Harry said. "I know where we can get good steaks."

This was how we wound up at The Bakery on Niagara Street.

§§§

A casual steakhouse and in a small way a sports bar, The Bakery had a décor that was comfortably old-fashioned. The dining room had wallpaper with floral stipes on which hung wood-framed pictures of women from the 1890s. Red and white floral tablecloths continued the theme, and low floor lamps with fringed hoods stood near the tables. Against the wall was an antique wood credenza lined with old stonecast pottery. A chalkboard on a maple-stained post announced the day's specials.

We were led down a flight of four stairs to a corner table in the back. The guys ordered beers to start with.

"Gonna have steak, you need a good lager to go with it," my gourmet-sleuth friend instructed.

Harry agreed. "Enhances the flavor."

"I see," I said.

Rebecca and I ordered wine—a good red wine enhances the flavor of everything.

While we waited for our meat to grill, Roger recapped his interrogation of Stonemaiden. When he finished, Harry asked, "So what do you make of what you heard, Detective?"

"Has to be one of the band members— maybe all of 'em. Being in town just when our victim bought it…" He shook his head. "Uh-uh. Can't see it as a coincidence."

"What about that lawyer? He looks… sleazy," Rebecca said.

Harry put down his beer, and laughed. "That your considered opinion?"

My friend's cheeks grew flushed. "Well… The perfect way he was dressed, and that slicked-back hair… I didn't trust him."

"Not to mention the fact he has loose lips," I said. "Remember, he all but told Grace Linden what was in Amanda's Will."

"I agree he's not the best lawyer in town," Harry said. "But he's been here for years and never got caught doing anything illegal."

"Besides," Roger added, "what would be his motive for killing Stone? Her money? If he'd wanted that, he would've grabbed it after she was dead. Never said anything to Grace, never told you or the band she left anything behind. No, good lawyer or bad, the man's not stupid enough to make that kind of mistake."

A waiter in black pants and a white shirt brought our meals. Steaks, potatoes and creamed spinach.

While slicing into his ribeye, Harry said, "That leaves the band."

"Them, and their manager, Eric Riley," Roger replied.

"Think it could be him?"

"I don't know. Maybe. Even at his age, he could've shot Stone then arranged the crime scene. Plus, his age could've played into her letting him into her house— probably wouldn't've been scared of him."

Rebecca dipped a fried potato into ketchup. "That's right," she said. "When we were leaving her house, Amanda told Emlyn she *needed* her. Now that I think about it, that sounded like she was afraid of someone."

"So, we come back to the band," Roger said. "They're as much a rough-and-tumble group as any I've come across. One day in town, and Simms, the bass player, and Louellen the guitarist, got into a bar fight up on Main Street. Either of 'em could have smashed his way in through the window, then fixed it so it'd look like our vic let her killer in.

"Then there's Bobby Davis," I said. "But, he's still in love with Amanda even after not seeing her for more than thirty years.

"Not sure I buy that story," Roger said.

"But, the way he cried when he talked about her…"

I admit I'm something of a romantic. At the end of each story I write, my heroine finds her love. Well, most of the time.

Still not able to believe the band she worshiped could do something this evil, my star-struck friend Rebecca said, "I believed him."

"Nah. His crying doesn't mean anything. Man's been on the stage as long as he has, he couldn't keep selling to audiences if he hasn't learned to act."

"And his motive?" Harry said.

"Motive's what I can't get past with any of 'em."

"You once told me the motive for these crimes comes down to love or money," I said. "Amanda leaving the band must have cost them a lot of money—cost their manager a bunch, also. Maybe this wasn't some kind of grand plan. When they arrived in Niagara Falls, they could have found out she was living here, and in a rage, went after her."

Roger patted my hand. "Good thought. But, there are two things wrong with the idea. First, how'd they find out Stone was here? It's not like she was advertising it."

"They could have read that *Gazette* article," I said with a slight sulk.

"The article was in the paper a couple of weeks ago, so I can't make it fly as bringing on sudden anger. More to the point, the scene didn't have the look of a crime of passion. A single bullet in her head? No, hatred—or vengeance—would have beaten her face in, or filled her body with lead."

Hesitantly, Rebecca offered, "Maybe this has nothing to do with Stonemaiden. Have you thought about that? Maybe a local thief broke in to rob Amanda."

"Looks like that could be," Harry said. "Drawers were rifled through downstairs and in her bedroom. I suppose we ought to check out other burglaries around the county, see if any of them has the same odor."

Still trying to find a key to unlock a motive that would define a killer, we started back to my house after dessert. If only we'd found that key before we left the restaurant.

Chapter Eight
What's Hidden Must Be Found

In the front seat, next to Roger, Harry spotted it first.

We'd just passed the Nelson's house—my neighbors to the right—when he tapped Roger's shoulder, and almost in a whisper said, "Slow down."

Roger glanced sideways at him.

Harry pointed to my front door.

"What is it?" Rebecca asked.

I rolled down my backseat window, and gasped. My front door was wide open.

Roger pulled his SUV onto the dirt on the border between my front yard and the Nelson's.

Leaning over his seat, Harry said, "You ladies stay here!"

After climbing from the Trailblazer, Roger walked behind the back of his car, and tapped the front passenger door. Crouched, their pistols drawn and at their sides, he and Harry moved quickly to my house. In moments, side-by-side, they stood up with their backs against the wall. Now Harry pointed to himself, then, making a signal like feet walking, he pointed to the fence enclosing my backyard. Next he pointed at Roger, then the front door, and held up five fingers. Roger gave a slight nod, and watched as his boss opened the gate and scooted into my yard. Seconds later, bent at the waist Roger ran below my front window and into my house.

I held my breath, waiting to hear gunshots; praying if I heard shots, they wouldn't hurt either of these men Rebecca and I cared so much about. I hoped my friend was correct about a witch's thoughts having the effect of a spell.

Five minutes passed. Ten minutes. At last, Harry came through the door. I released my breath, and heard my friend release hers.

He walked to my driveway, then down to the street where he looked up and down River Road. Just where the road bends toward North Tonawanda, a car sped away. For a minute, Harry stared after it. Finally, he walked back to where Rebecca and I sat in the SUV.

"It's all clear inside," he said. "You can go in."

While he helped my friend, I rushed to my house.

Roger grabbed my arm as I came through the door." Holding on tight, he said. "Brace yourself. You're not gonna like what you see."

I stiffened, and peered over his shoulder. My over-stuffed chair had been toppled; its cushions and those from my sofa had been tossed. One of the cushions had been slashed. Books from my bookcases were scattered. I looked past this mess, and saw my French door was broken, the glass panes shattered. I looked to my right. All my kitchen cabinets were open, dishes and pots thrown to the floor and on the counter.

I slipped from Roger's arms to the floor, and bawled.

At that moment, Rebecca came in. "Oh my God!" she said. "It'll take weeks to straighten all this—" She stopped in mid-sentence, obviously struck by another thought. "Where's… Sarah's book?"

I'd been so shocked by the mess someone made of my home, I hadn't thought of my ancestor's book. I'd left it on my desk. I jumped to my feet, and tore into the living room. My desk was a mess, the drawers pulled out, paper every-where.

"Where is it?" I cried.

A white head poked out from under the desk. Thank goodness whoever did this hadn't hurt Elvira. I knelt to pick up my cat—a struggle with my ribs still sore. Beneath her was the old book. Obviously, this wonderful, smart cat had heard the French door break, run to my desk, knocked

Sarah's book to the floor, and sat on it until we came home. I could think of no other explanation.

While I stood with the book in my arms and the cat curled-up next to my legs, I heard the guys talking in the kitchen.

"Car down the road took off," Harry said.

"See who was in it?"

"Nah. Only caught enough of the license place to see it was a rental. Too far away to tell from where."

A moment later, I saw Harry peer into my living room. "Leave out the body," he said, "this looks like the other place."

"That's what's got me worried," Roger said. I heard his footsteps in the hall. "I'm thinking someone wanted something Stone had, and now they think Emlyn's got it."

"Let's haul the bunch of them in and stay on them until one of them cracks." Harry dropped his voice to a whisper. That, and what he said next, caused me to shiver. "Better park Collins out front. Whichever of them is doing this isn't above killing."

A few minutes later, Roger came into the living room. "Rebecca's brewing some of her stuff. Woody and I are going to have a long conversation with Stonemaiden and their manager."

Tears in my eyes, I looked up and him.

He stroked my hair. "You and Rebecca are gonna stay tucked in here. Right?

I nodded.

"Good girl." He lifted my chin and looked into my eyes. "I wouldn't want to lose you."

As he and Harry left my house, Roger said to Rebecca, "Give her plenty of whatever you're making—maybe mix some whisky in it. I'll have an officer here to watch out for you in a half hour or so."

§§§

By the time my friend brought mugs of tea into the living room, Elvira had pulled a sofa cushion under the coffee table and settled against it for a nap. I was on the floor near my desk with old Sarah's book open on my lap.

"The guys picked up the things in the kitchen," Rebecca said.

I didn't respond.

"They dragged a trash bag with the broken dishes out to the curb."

I turned a page in the book.

"We should straighten up in here."

I turned another page.

The crutches under her arms, Rebecca dropped her hands on her hips. "Emlyn, you can't spend the rest of your life on the floor feeling sorry for yourself. Get up. Do something."

"I *am* doing something," I said. "I'm searching for an answer."

She groaned. "Don't you learn? You heard Roger—the guys are gonna pull Stonemaiden in and question them. Let them do their job!"

My finger on the passage I'd been reading, I looked up at her. "You saw the way all of them behaved in Kline's office when Roger questioned them. They won't say a thing without their lawyer in the room, and *he* won't let them say anything. Then Roger and Harry will have to let them go, and we'll be back where we are now." I waved my hand around the room. "I need an idea that'll tell us which one of them did this."

My cat lifted her head from the pillow and nodded

"Tell *us*?" Rebecca shouted. "No, no, no!" She leaned down and tapped the cast on her leg. "You're not dragging me into another one of your ideas. And you, Elvira, stop encouraging her!"

I dropped my eyes to Sarah's book. "I'm not doing the dragging this time. One of those people at Kline's office did this. And, in case you haven't noticed, whichever it is, is already coming after us."

Rebecca looked up at the ceiling, and groaned, "Why me, God? What did I ever do that was so bad, you brought *her* into my life?" With a sigh, she leaned on her crutch, and grabbed the cushion from underneath Elvira. "Well, if I'm gonna get killed, I might as well see what direction the bullet's coming from. Help me put your sofa back together. I can't sit on the floor."

At another time I might have argued with her. Not now. Rattled—Mom might not have been Mom, and my home had been invaded—I couldn't focus. I laid the book aside, and used my desk chair to pull myself up.

It took the rest of the evening to straighten the sofa and chair, and set my books back in the bookcases. By then, Officer Collins was parked in my driveway. Feeling safer than I had since Roger and Harry left, I dropped my guard enough to let weariness creep up on me. What a lovely voice my bed had when it called my name. As I headed upstairs, Rebecca again sighed. This time it had to be with relief. I'd have bet she'd calculated if she kept me busy cleaning long enough, I'd fall into a stupor and she'd be safe. At least, for that night.

§§§

Eight hours of vague dreams behind me, early the next morning I was dressed, and on the sofa with Sarah's *Book of Shadows*. An hour later, Rebecca came downstairs. Cabinet doors in the kitchen opened and closed. Grumbling, she came into the living room, and stood in front of me.

"Can't make coffee," she said. "Even your pot was broken."

"I noticed," I said, and returned my attention to the book.

"Still hoping your ancient relative will tell you something?"

"She has in the past."

"Well… scooch over. Maybe I can help."

I smiled at her. "Not still afraid I'll drag you into something dangerous?"

She shrugged. "No coffee, what other excitement do I have in my life."

After more than an hour of struggling to decipher the badly faded text, and words in which "S"s looked like "F"s and "A"s were placed where "I"s should have been, we stumbled across an entry. Frustrated, I handed the magnifying glass to Rebecca. "Can you figure out what Sarah's saying?"

She struggled with the text as I had, until, at last, she was able to read this much:

14 May, in the year of our Lord, 1692.

Dreary grows this cell of after so many days. I lay on straw counting the hours until I perish. I am brought to this time by The Old One, so evil none dare speak his name lest he turn his eyes upon them and they will be as I, condemned. What potion might I brew to dispel him and be spared from Gallows Hill? It is acacia that I need to seek illumination, and know by whose name Satan has been summoned. Then, with the root of archangel I might exorcise this evil. But Magistrate Corwin has given the evil in this Salem Town my name, and Judge Cotton Mather's Court of Oyer and Terminer has ordered him to lock away these plants by which I would find the truth—

My eyes had been closed while I listened to my friend read. Now they popped open.

"Wait!" I said. "Read that again—the last part."

She did.

I sat forward. "That's it!"

"What's it? *Oooh*, Emlyn, I hate when you do this."

I stood, and handed the crutches to her. "Come on."

"Where?"

As I rushed to the kitchen, I mumbled, "How stupid I've been!"

She thump-stepped, thump-stepped after me. "What are you talking about?"

I picked up my purse. "Locked away. Yes, that has to be the answer."

She stared at me with a blank expression.

"Locked away," I repeated. "Don't you see? The key." I reached into my purse, and took out the key Howard Kline had given me. "This! It'll unlock everything. Or, at least, it'll open Amanda's safe deposit box. We have to see what's in it."

"Uh-uh." Rebecca stamped her foot (stamped her crutch, actually). "Roger said we're supposed to stay here."

I moved to the front door. "What he meant is that he wants us where Office Collins can keep an eye on us.

"Yeah."

"So, we'll take Collins with us."

"But, you don't know where Amanda's safe deposit box is," Rebecca objected.

"Sure I do. It's in the Bank of America on Military Road."

She grabbed my shoulder. "Have you suddenly gone clairvoyant? That can happen to a witch that's tried as many clairvoyance spells as you have—sometimes they can't get rid of it."

I laughed. "If only. No. I recognize the key. I have a box in the same location. Now, let's go."

As I opened the door, I heard the patter of feet behind me. In seconds, Elvira was looking up at me with a pleading expression that said, *Don't leave me here alone.*

"Stop it, you big wuss."

She wrapped her front paws around my leg and *meowwwed*, which I took to mean, *No! The killer will get me.*

I had no choice. I lifted the big lump, and headed outside.

"I don't have a good feeling about this," Rebecca said as she followed me to out. She continued to mutter all the way to the driveway.

Ignoring her, I tapped on the window of the patrol car.

The young cop was less thrilled by my plan than was my friend. When I asked him to drive us to the bank, he shook his head with such vehemence, I feared it would topple from his shoulders and roll down River Road.

"No!" he said. "Uh-uh. The detective instructed me to watch you *here*. No way I'm going to disobey a direct order."

I pleaded with the man to no effect, until, at last, I said, "Call Roger. Tell him I have the key to Amanda Stone's safe deposit box, and what's in it will tell us who the killer is."

"Please, Ms. Goode, don't make me tell him that," Collins said. "He'll think I've gone nuts and dump me off the force."

Anxious, because someone who thought I had what was in that box might still be out there, I hissed, "Just do it!"

In my arms, Elvira pawed his hand.

"Hey. Your cat's scratching me."

I held Elvira out. "Call Roger or I'll let her do worse."

The threat of my cat going after other parts of him was sufficient. Collins pulled a cellphone from his uniform pocket, and punched in some numbers. When Roger answered, he said, "Sorry to bother you, Detective, but the lady, uh... and her cat insisted."

I heard Roger's deep baritone laugh. A second later, Collins gave me a sideways glance, and said, "Yes, sir. She certainly is."

With a growl, I grabbed the phone. "Keep laughing at me, you big lummox, I'll turn you into something even my cat won't eat."

"Okay, okay." He kept laughing. "What do you want from Collins?"

I explained where he had to take us, and why?

Roger was quiet for a moment, then said, "Might not be a bad idea, Emlyn. What's in that box might be something to push these characters the Chief and I have been talking to all night."

I handed the phone back to Collins, who listened, then said, "Yes, sir."

Chapter Nine
The Box

The Bank of America branch was on Military Road, behind a Sunoco station and a Marco's Pizza shop. With the cat in my arms, and Rebecca and Officer Collins on either side of me, I strolled to the glass cubicles to the right of the tellers.

A woman seated at one of the desks looked up. "Hi, Emlyn. What can we do for you today?"

"I need to get into one of the boxes, Fern."

She laughed. "Gonna put Elvira away for safe keeping?"

I laughed, too. "*Hmm.* Not a bad idea."

My cat growled, clearly not amused by what I thought to be a rather good joke

I handed Fern the key.

Rapidly running her fingers over the computer keyboard on her desk, she brought up the information. Pointing to her screen, she said, "The owner of this box is Amanda Stone."

"I know, but—"

"No. It's okay. I see you down as a co-owner."

Now, she glanced at the uniformed cop who hovered just outside her cubicle. From her expression, she might have wondered if I had been hiding illicit drugs in her bank's safe deposit vault.

Collins cleared his throat. "Ms. Goode is helping us with an official investigation."

I shuddered. Though I was sure he meant well, his words had probably shoved my reputation onto the *Gazette's* page that told who in town had been arrested.

With a nod and not another word, Fern rose and led us through the door behind the tellers. In the vault, she pointed to the box I'd come for—a fairly large box—then stood by the door, perhaps waiting to see what jack would pop out of that box.

I also wondered what was in it, and was half-afraid to find out. Could the contents of the box on the table before me have gotten Amanda Stone killed? Could having it get me killed? I gave Elvira to Officer Collins. My hand shaking, I turned the key. With Rebecca and Collins leaning over my shoulders, I peeked inside.

"What's this?" I said.

Rebecca picked up the flat, square cardboard carton—the only item Amanda had put in her safe deposit box—and said, "I think this is a tape recording."

"You mean Stone taped someone's conversation, and that's what got her killed?" Collins said.

Elvira *mewed*, as if to say, *Sticking her nose in, got it chopped off.*

"You're right, cat," I said. "If she'd bugged someone's phone and caught him talking about a crime he committed, that certainly would've done it."

Elvira looked at me with a smug expression; Collins stared at me as if I'd lost my mind.

Rebecca turned the carton over. Her lips moving, she silently read what was written on the other side.

"No," my friend said. "It's not that kind of tape. This is… Look."

She pointed to the label affixed to the carton. Yellowed with age, the label said THE RECORD MACHINE.

"That's the studio Stonemaiden recorded in. I know 'cause the name's on their album jackets. And see these? They're song titles. But they aren't on any record the band ever released." Rebecca opened the carton. "Oh. God!" she said. "A quarter-inch tape. I've seen one of these—a customer at my shop made some records at the Mammoth Recoding Studios in Buffalo. This could be the album people said Stonemaiden recorded but never released."

Carefully, my friend closed the carton, then held it against her chest, as if it were a long lost treasure. Which, in a sense, it was. This square, flat box could contain the band's ticket on a space shuttle flight back to the stars. Would it be worth killing for? In the time I'd spent with Roger, I'd witnessed people kill for a lot less.

Bless Sarah Goode and her *Book of Shadows*. Once again, she had pointed me in the right direction.

I pulled my cellphone from my purse, and punched in Roger's number. As soon as I heard his voice, I said, "You'll never guess what we found. Go on, guess."

Hey, a girl's entitled to preen now and then, isn't she?

He sighed. "I don't have time for games right now, Emlyn. If you have something to say, tell me. Otherwise, I have to get back to the interrogation."

"You're no fun, you know that?"

"Emlyn!"

"Oh, all right." I told him what the safe deposit box contained.

Immediately, his voice lightened. "I believe you've just handed me my motive. Good girl. Now, put Collins on."

I pushed the button to make my device a speaker-phone, and handed it to the officer.

"I'm here, Detective."

"Take the ladies right home—no detours—then bring me the tape. And Collins, guard it with your life."

Guard the tape with his life? What about Rebecca and me?

I snatched back my phone. "Hey, you big lug. If Collins brings you the tape... What if the killer comes back to my house?"

"Won't happen," Roger said. "We've got the case wrapped up. We're gonna hold Davis for the murder—and for trashing your house. We've let the others go. So, go home. I'll be there in a little while. Oh, and tell Rebecca I'm sorry this wrecks her plans to see a Stonemaiden concert."

All right, problem solved, case closed, I'll be able to sleep tonight. But...

A pesty gnat of doubt started to flit about me. Try as I might, I couldn't swat it away.

Chapter Ten
Damn Pesty Gnat

Next to Rebecca in the back of Collins's squad car, over and over, I said, "It's the wrong answer. I'm missing some-thing. What am I missing?"

My friend shoved me. "What are you groaning about, now?"

I stared out the window. "It doesn't... feel right."

"What doesn't?"

"It can't be Bobby Davis. The pieces of this jigsaw puzzle don't belong there."

The look Collins gave me earlier—the one where he wondered if the redhead in the bank vault had gone nuts? He looked in the rearview mirror at me now with the same expression.

"I don't want it to be him, either," Rebecca said. "But, Roger—"

"He has it wrong."

She pulled on her long salt and pepper braid. "Well, if not Bobby, who?"

Again I moaned. "I don't know. There's a piece I'm missing. I know I saw something, heard something... Damn! Why can't I remember?"

"Maybe it's something you heard in that lawyer's office… Hey, maybe it's the lawyer. I told you I don't trust him. He's sleazy looking."

While watching the traffic flow along Niagara Falls Boulevard, I said, "I suppose Kline could be responsible. He knew Amanda had a safe deposit box, and since she had one, there had to be something of value she put in it."

"And he gave you the key, because only you could open the box," Rebecca prompted. "And then he searched through you house because he thought you'd brought the treasure home."

Following her line of reasoning, I said, "And he killed Amanda, because that was the only way to get me the key. It's possible, but… No. Once he got the tape, what could he do with it?"

"Sell it, of course."

"Uh-uh. That would start the police investigating how he got it."

"Well, I still don't trust him. But, okay, if not him, one of the band members?"

I thought about this. *Could I be wrong about Bobby Davis? I discounted him only because I believe he loves Amanda, even after not seeing her for thirty years. Still, love spurned can turn to hate—I've read stories built on that theme.* This thought let to another. *Roger loves me. If I run out on him and he finds me after so many years, would he kill me?*

Wondering what Roger might do got me no closer to the missing puzzle piece. I had to concentrate.

So, Bobby Davis.

"How would Davis have known Amanda lived in Niagara Falls," I wondered aloud. "Stumbling over her here would be too coincidental for anything but one of my stories. Whoever killed her must have not only known she lived here, he knew what she'd hidden away. Why else would he have ransacked both her house and mine?"

Collins stopped at the light at Williams Road, just across from the airport. With a glance over his shoulder at us, he asked, "Could it have been any of the other band members?"

"I don't think so," I said. "Even though they didn't love Stone the way Davis did, the problem is still the same. How would they know she lived in—" I stopped in mid-sentence.

His attention back on the road, Collins made the right turn on Williams, and headed past the Summit Mall.

Rebecca leaned over, and looked in my eyes. "You know who did it, don't you."

I nodded. The stupid gnat that had been bugging me (pardon the pun), finally flew off. "The facts fit only one person," I said. "It has to be him."

"Who?" Rebecca demanded.

"I'm such an idiot! That entry Sarah made, as much as told me who killed Amanda. Why did it take me so long to see?"

"*Oooh*, Emlyn Goode. Sometimes I hate you enough to kill *you*—or at least hit you with a spell that'll make you stutter."

"You can't do spells, remember? Witchcraft isn't in your genes."

She smacked my arm. "Who. Is. It!"

Elvira shot me a pink-eyed glare. Her expression seemed to say, *You can, at least, tell me!*

I held up my index finger, and grabbed the cellphone from my purse.

Obviously, Roger saw my phone number come up on Caller ID. Before I could say hello, he said, "What is it now, Emlyn?"

This was too important to be annoyed by his abrupt-ness. Very calmly, I said, "You're holding the wrong guy."

"Are we?"

I heard concern in his voice. Roger and I had run along this road before. He knew I wouldn't make such a state-ment if I weren't sure. "Eric Riley killed Amanda." I said. "If I were you, I'd haul him back in before that fish slips off your line."

As he made the left onto River Road, Collins's jaw dropped.

Rebecca gasped.

Elvira's *meow* sounded like a giggle.

Roger laughed. "Did you have to say that like in a potboiler novel?"

"Sorry," I said. "I've been reading Marlon James's *The Book of Night Women*." I made a mental note to not let what I read crawl into how I spoke. "Okay. You'll want to get your hands on Riley. Better?"

"Better," he replied. "How do you know he's my perp?"

So, it's okay for you to talk like a detective novel? I thought. I didn't say it, because Roger *is* a detective. "I'll tell you later. Right now—"

"Yeah, yeah," he said. "I'll get some cars after him…" He hesitated. "If the guy's smart, he'll be halfway to the airport by now. Still, be very careful when you get home. You never know. And tell Collins to forget about bringing me the tape. I want him to stay with you and Rebecca."

§§§

Five minutes later the patrol car pulled into my driveway.

As I opened the door and slid from the backseat, I said, "Collins, thanks for being our guardian angel all day."

He smiled. "My pleasure, ma'am."

I leaned down at his window. "Ma'am makes me sound like an old woman. Call me Emlyn."

His smile widened.

I thought for a second, then said, "I don't want to keep calling you Collins. What's your first name?"

He turned off the ignition. "Peter," he said. "But, my friends call me Irish."

"Well, Irish," Rebecca said. "How about coming in for some coffee?"

"I'd like that. Give me a minute. First I want to check around back—never can be too careful." He handed Rebecca the box holding Amanda's tape. "Don't wanna leave this in the car."

As we came through my front door, I put Elvira down in the hall. Immediately her hair bristled, her back arched, and she emitted a sound that was as much a screech as a growl.

Rebecca and I both froze, staring at the cat.

"I think somebody's in here," I whispered.

"I know," she said. "You should call for Irish."

"First we have to get out of here."

I stooped to pick up Elvira, but didn't quite get my hands on her. With a screech that truly was one, she raced toward the living room. I straightened up, ready to chase after my feline friend. As I took my first step, I heard a shouted, "Get away from me, ya stupid cat!" A second later she flew across the room, and lay, stunned, against my bookcases. Eric Riley moved from the alcove where I do my writing, and stood in the hall, facing us. In his right hand, he held a pistol. I have no idea what kind it was. I could only see its very large size.

"What do you want?" I said—a stupid question.

"Shut up. Don't move." Riley's white hair was a mess and his wrinkled suit had grass stains. He looked as if he'd crawled through my back yard, trying to remain unseen.

I didn't need to do any research to learn one didn't argue with a man holding a gun. I shut my mouth.

"Just give me that tape," he said, "and no one needs to get hurt."

Gun or no gun, I wasn't able to remain silent too long. That was genetic, I think. My mother also had that problem.

"You mean, no one else, don't you." I said. "Did you have to kill Amanda?"

Rebecca smacked my leg with her crutch. "He said to shut up. You wanna get us shot?"

I stared at him. "I want to know. Did you have to?"

"She stole the tape from the studio before she ran off," Riley said. "I just went to her house to get it back. By rights, it mine."

"It belongs to the band."

His laugh was more evil than any I'd ever heard. "The band," he said. "What do they know? Bunch of morons. All they want is to be playing their instruments or fighting in bars. They've got no idea how much this tape is worth."

"And you do?" I said.

"*Shhh*!" Rebecca held out the box. "Let's just give this to him so he'll leave."

Riley grabbed the tape box from her. "This is worth enough to set me up in comfort for the years I've got left."

"At Kline's office," I said, "You told us you already had enough to keep you in cigars that long."

"You know what Havanas cost these days?" Again he made that horrid laugh. "Okay, enough of this. Been nice chatting with you, but I've gotta go. *Hasta la vista*, ladies." He raised his pistol.

Just as he began to apply pressure to the trigger, what was left of my French door crashed in. Behind the debris, Collins stood with one foot on the patio and his other in my living room. His service revolver drawn, he shouted, "Drop your weapon!"

Riley turned on him, clearly not ready to surrender.

"No you don't!" Rebecca said.

I heard a swish and saw a blur move past me. The next thing I knew, Riley was face-down on the floor, holding his head. Rebecca stood over him with her crutch raised and ready to hit him again.

Collins lowered his pistol. In seconds he had Riley handcuffed. Then he stood, and wiped his brow with the back of his hand. "What did you say before about a guardian angel?"

Chapter Eleven
Final Puzzle Pieces

Eric Riley was arraigned the next morning. At the arraign-ment, Howard Kline argued fervently that, at his age, the man was not a flight-risk. When the lawyer finished his argument, Judge Aldernado shook his head, and ruled that if ever he'd seen a case in which a man should be locked up and the key thrown in an incinerator, this was it. So, Riley now sat in the Niagara County jail, awaiting his trial.

The Amanda Stone matter behind us, Harry assigned Officer Collins—whom we now called Irish—to chauffeur Rebecca and me to the Military Road Outlet Mall so I could replace my broken dishes. When I thanked Harry, he gave me his half-smile, and said, "Don't thank *me*. The kid volunteered."

While we ran this errand, Roger sat in my living room, where he supervised the carpenters who replaced my French door. Not to be left out, Harry went to Sam's Club to buy food (need I say Rebecca and I ate steak for weeks afterward?). Now, our errands competed and dinner cooked, five of us—Roger, Harry, Rebecca, me, and Irish Collins—sat around my dinette table, enjoying our steaks, potatoes, and creamed spinach. Though a bit crowded (the round table was made to seat four) we were comfortable and content.

Elvira sat on the floor beside the table, not looking terribly comfortable with her paw taped where it had been broken when that SOB threw her across my living room.

While Harry sliced the cherry pie he bought us for desert, he said, "There are still two things I haven't figured out about this case."

"Only two?" Roger said.

Harry laughed. "Careful, Detective. It's not smart to make fun of a man who can assign you to counting cars on Pine Avenue."

"Yes, sir." Roger gave him a cockeyed salute.

Irish tried hard to hide a grin.

"Seriously," Harry said. "Why did Amanda Stone leave the band and the high life that went with it?"

"That's easy," Rebecca said. "She told us the day we visited her. At a party before her last concert, she was raped."

Harry thought for a second, then said, "I understand what a trauma such a thing is. But, not every woman who suffers that runs away from a career she's taken years to build."

Roger touched my wrist. "I can figure this one. The rapist had to be someone involved with Stonemaiden. That's why she couldn't keep performing with them."

I acknowledged this statement with a smile, and added, "Amanda actually told us who did it?"

"She did?" the others at the table said almost in unison.

I nodded. "It wouldn't have been Bobby Davis—she and he were already sleeping together. And Simms and Louellen really had little interest in her. So it had to be Riley."

"Good reasoning," Roger said. "But, you just told us Stone pointed to her rapist."

"Yeah, she did. When Howard Kline was reading her Will, he told us Amanda had instructed him to tell Riley 'thanks for the ride'. What else could she have meant by that?"

"Okay, I get why she left the band and how you knew who raped her," Harry said. "But I still don't follow how you figured out Riley killed her."

"Oh, that," I said. "Roger, you told us from the beginning that Stonemaiden being in Niagara Falls just when Amanda was killed couldn't have been a coincidence. It had to follow, then, that they had deliberately taken the booking to get close to her. It took me awhile to realize there's only one way they could have known she was here."

"They could've read about her in the Gazette," Irish said.

"No, that story was printed weeks ago, and it wouldn't have gotten downstate. So, as I said, there's just one way any of them could have known, and at the same time, it meant only one of them *would* have known."

Harry tossed his napkin on his plate. "Are you going to tell us?"

Stroking his cheek, Rebecca said, "She did the same thing to me while Irish drove us home from the bank. I was ready to open the door and push her out."

"Can't you give a girl a chance?" I said.

Roger grumbled.

"Okay. Someone at the casino must have called to book the band up here, and it had to be Riley, their manager, who got the call. In fact, I'll bet the casino's booker told him Amanda lived here, and suggested it would be a major event if she joined them for a reunion concert."

Of course, I didn't mention that Sarah Goode had as much as told me Riley was the devil in this case, when I read what she wrote on May 14, 1692. That entry in her

Book of Shadows said the Devil was the Old One.

Dinner finished, Harry began to gather the dishes.

"Rebecca and I can clean up," I said.

Harry shook his head. "You and Becca have had a rough couple of days."

"Yeah, go relax," Roger said. "We've got this."

I grinned. My friend reached for her crutches. If these guys wanted to spoil us a bit, neither she nor I intended to argue with them.

Settled on the sofa in my living room, we stared through my new French door at the sun setting over the stand of trees that guarded the Niagara River. After about ten minutes, Rebecca turned to me.

"You still haven't resolved that business about whether Amanda Stone was your mother."

I nodded. I'd been thinking about this all day.

She pointed to my desk, where Sarah Goode's book was safely tucked away in a drawer. "I hate to suggest this, but there's a way you could try to find out."

"A spell to travel back to when I was born?" I said.

"Well, you did it a few weeks ago, and it sorta worked."

"Uh-huh. And what it led to landed us both in the hospital. No. I think I'll stay where I am... at least, for a while. Anyway, I've decided it doesn't really matter who gave birth to me. As difficult a child as I was, Anne Goode was always there for me. I can live with that."

I thought for a moment, then added, "Besides, you met my mother. Who else's genes could I have?"

Susan Lynn Solomon

Formerly a Manhattan entertainment attorney and a contributing editor to the quarterly art magazine SunStorm Fine Art, Susan Lynn Solomon now lives in Niagara Falls, New York/

Since 2007 many of her short stories have appeared in literary journals, including, *Abigail Bender* (awarded an Honorable Mention in a short romance competition), *Ginger Man, Elvira, The Memory Tree, Going Home, Yesterday's Wings, Smoker's Lament, Kaddish,* and *Sabbath* (nominated for *2013 Best of the Net*). A collection of her short stories, *Voices In My Head*, has been published by Solstice Publishing.

A finalist in M&M's Chanticleer's Mystery & Mayhem Novel Contest, and a finalist for the 2016 Book Excellence Award, Susan Lynn Solomon's first Solstice Publishing novel, *The Magic of Murder*, has received rave reviews, as has the novelette, *Bella Vita*, and the novel, *Dead Again* all stories that continue the adventures (and often missteps) of these characters. In the new Emlyn Goode Mystery novelette, *The Day the Music Died*, Ms. Solomon once more demonstrates that murder can have sense of humor.

Social media links

Facebook:
http://www.facebook.com/susanlynnsolomon
LinkedIn:
https://www.linkedin.com/in/susan-solomon-8183b129
Website: http://www.susanlynnsolomon.com
Twitter:
https://twitter.com/susanlynnsolom1
@susanlynnsolom1

If you enjoyed this story, check out these other Solstice Publishing mysteries by Susan Lynn Solomon:

Emlyn Goode Mysteries

The Magic of Murder

When his partner is discovered in a frozen alley with eight bullets in his chest, Niagara Falls Police Detective Roger Frey swears vengeance. But Detective Chief Woodward has forbidden him or anyone else on the detective squad to work the case. Emlyn Goode knows Roger will disobey his boss, which will cost him his job and his freedom. Because she cares for him more than she'll admit, she needs to stop him. Desperate, she can think of but one way.

Emlyn recently learned she's a direct descendant of a woman hanged as a witch in 1692. She has a book filled with arcane recipes and chants passed down through her family. Possessed of, or perhaps by a vivid imagination, she intends to use these to solve Jimmy's murder before Roger takes revenge on the killer. But she's new to this "witch thing," and needs help from her friend Rebecca Nurse, whose ancestor also took a short drop from a Salem tree. Rebecca's not much better at deciphering the ancient directions, and while the women stumble over spell after spell, the number possible killers grows. When Chief Woodward's wife is shot and a bottle bomb bursts through Emlyn's window, it becomes clear she's next on the killer's list.

https://bookgoodies.com/a/B015OQO5LO

Bella Vita

A car burns in the parking lot behind Bella Vita Hair Salon. The corpse in the front seat has a short sword pushed into his ribs. Beneath the car is a cast-iron cauldron filled with flowers. This seems to be a sacrificial rite Rebecca Nurse had been teaching Emlyn Goode. But is it? The corpse has been identified as George Malone, and earlier on this summer solstice day, he and his wife had severe argument. Could it be that Angela Malone has murdered her husband? Prodded by Elvira, an overly-large albino cat that wants the case solved so she can get some sleep, to Rebecca's dismay Emlyn again dips into her ancient relatives *Book of*

Shadows to find the answer before her friend and neighbor, Detective Roger Fry, can.

Dead Again

When Emlyn Goode's mother returns to Niagara Falls for a high school reunion, so does murder. During the reunion, a woman's body is found in the ladies room. Is this killing connected to one that occurred 40 years before in the woods below the town of Lewiston? Harry Woodward, a young police officer working his first murder case suspected Emlyn's mother of the crime, although there wasn't enough evidence to arrest her.

Home from a year-long leave, Harry—now the Niagara Falls Chief of Detectives—together with Emlyn's friend, Detective Roger Frey, investigates the latest killing. Distraught over indications her mother might have been involved in both murders, Emlyn, with her cohort, Rebecca Nurse, sets out to prove otherwise. But, danger lurks in the shadows when amateurs—even ones with witchy skills—get involved with murder.

Short Stories

The Memory Tree

In Central Florida, Farrell's Orchards is no longer what it had once been. Deborah Hannel knows this. She and her sister, Leah, grew up here, raised by their Aunt Harriet and Uncle Max. Uncle Max is gone now, as is Leah's husband; as are the husbands of several cousins. It seems divorce is as much a family tradition as Deborah's oyster stuffing, and bringing new ornaments to hang on the Christmas tree. When Deborah arrives alone for Christmas at Farrell's Orchards, will the ornament she's brought to hang on the tree be a memory of another impending divorce?

Captive Soul

Emily Marks grew up in Kew Gardens Hills—a nice neighborhood of middle class houses and neat yards. Except for the derelict house on the corner of Main Street next to the church.

Two badly weathered stories, slats rotting on the wrap-around porch, and the roof hanging by a few shingles in spots, this house was a neighborhood legend. The ghost of its murdered owner roamed its rooms, moaning with the wind on stormy nights. Cold fingers grabbed the living who dared to enter, and closed on their throats. That's what the high school kids told Emily and her friends.

She was ten, and frightened by the story. But when her friends dared her to join them in breaking to the house…well, only a ten-year-old wussy could turn down such a dare.

Now, seventeen years later, Emily must recount what happened that day and what's happened to her since. Her life depends on getting a psychiatrist to understand a ghost can attach itself to the living.

Collection

Voices In My Head

In The Magic of Murder, Susan Lynn Solomon let readers laugh at the antics of an albino cat and a witch. Now, in nine short tales she takes a serious look at relationships and their impact on characters who confront their pasts.

A young soldier returns, changed by his war. A young British girl faces the people of her town after parental abuse. An older man who as a teenager fled his hometown, returns when his childhood girlfriend begs a favor. A radical of the '70s leaves the cemetery after her mother's funeral, searching for where her life will lead.

In these stories and five others, Solomon explores the persistence of memory and the promise of hope.

Made in the USA
Middletown, DE
14 February 2020